CHANNEL

Issue 1 | Autumn 2019

Editors
Cassia Gaden Gilmartin
Elizabeth Murtough

Design & Layout
Cassia Gaden Gilmartin
Elizabeth Murtough

Published in Dublin, Ireland by *Channel*.
Printed by City Print Limited.

Cover art by Rachel Doolin.

Channel is published twice a year (April and October).

ISBN 978-1-9162245-0-6

Connect with us: www.channelmag.org | info@channelmag.org
facebook.com/ChannelLiteraryMagazine/ | twitter: @Channel_LitMag | instagram: @channel_mag

Fiction

13	Jan Carson	Florence, Oregon
30	John Creevy	In the Garden
63	Don Ó Donnacháin	Derry 2084: A Burial
85	Michael Phoenix	The Dogs

Essay

40	Polly Waterfield	Bones

Poetry

1	John Paul Davies	Sea Swell
3	Joey Lew	As Alive
4		In My Backyard
5	Grace Wilentz	Belly of the Whale
7	Rosamund Taylor	On the Lichens and Liverwort of Bantry Bay
11		No Natural Predators
23	D.S. Maolalai	Crabs and Netted Mackerel
25		Dandelion Clocks
26	Martina Dalton	The Actual Stag
28	Elspeth Wilson	We cannot eat hares
29	Colin Hopkirk	Buzzard
31	Patrick Deeley	Begun Things
33	Amanda Bell	Dodder River Haiku

35	Lucy Crispin	January sends a short but important memo
36	Ojo Taiye	at the age of four
38	Suzzanna Matthews	Hope Arise
52	Karen O'Connor	Field of Gulls
53	Lisa Stice	Incidental
54	Lola Scollard	Life, Still with Pheasant
56	Iain Twiddy	Shannon
57	Lydia Unsworth	Nothing That Understands Stays Silent
59		Chestnuts
61	David Butler	Annaghmakerrig
76	Anne McCrea	bog people
77	Seth Crook	Daily Swim
78	Mark Baker	Sunny Spell
79	Marc Swan	Wild About Wampum
81	Paul Lewis	Salthill Littoral
93	Toby Buckley	Inver
94	Aoife Riach	Priorities
95	Celia Claase	Cylinder Creature
96	Pete Mullineaux	Boarders
97	Lisa Reily	in a bath with Bruce Dawe
99	Cliona O'Connell	Tornado
100		Whites and Shadows
102		Notes on Contributors

Cover Image: Installation view of Fragility of Things, 2019, a mixed-media artwork created by visual artist Rachel Doolin
Image location: Stairwell Gallery Space, Uillinn, West Cork Arts Centre
Materials: Dandelion seed heads, Blackthorn
Dimensions: Variable

Fragility of Things, 2019

"Weeds are the boundary breakers, the stateless minority, who remind us that life is just not that tidy. They could help us learn to live across nature's borderlines again."

Richard Mabey, from 'Weeds'

Fragility of Things alludes to notions of hostility and survival in an escalating global crisis. A "Non-place" is a neologism coined by French anthropologist Marc Augé. It refers to anthropological spaces of transience, which do not hold enough significance to be regarded as places, where human beings remain anonymous. While gathering material for this installation I have found myself wandering in non-places; wastelands, derelict sites, roadsides and roundabouts. The unregarded territories where life thrives on the fringes, laying root in unsettled ground, obstructing our orderly maps of the world.

Writer Richard Mabey considers how the maligning of weeds as "undesirable outcasts" can be interpreted as a cultural signifier that shapes hostile attitudes towards our environment. This is a poignant metaphor that echoes current perspectives on migration.

In essence, The Fragility of Things responds to our rapidly changing world, where the devastating effects of ecological imbalance continue to bring uncertainty, trauma and loss to displaced populations globally.

Rachel Doolin, b.1981, is an emerging visual artist residing in the South of Ireland. Doolin's multifaceted practice marries art, experimentation and ecology to explore themes that often concern materiality, habitation and the environment. Employing a methodology of making that the artist describes as "simple complexity," Doolin gathers, manipulates and combines various media to realize her multi-layered and poetic provocations. Her sculptural and installation based works are simultaneously delicate and complex aggregations that pertain to the vulnerability and persistence, fragility and tenacity of life in the Anthropocene.

www.racheldoolin.com

Note from the Editors

In all uses of the word, a "channel" exists to direct something—an idea, a material, a spirit—through or towards something else. In nature, it may be a length of water that joins two seas or a navigable passage in waters otherwise unsafe for sailors. In electronics, a band of frequencies used for transmission. *Channel*, too, is intended as a means of communication, a passage for narratives, ideas and sentiments surrounding the natural world.

Our lives are imprinted by nature and, in turn, imprinted upon it. The scope of our articulation is defined by what we encounter and so, in English, every obstacle is a river to cross; every person trapped is a caged bird. We name the world with our whimsy: *Baby's Breath, Lady's Mantle, Granny's Bonnet*. Across the industrialised world, however, we are losing our connection to the reciprocity of this process which has, for millennia, shaped how we think, feel and communicate.

In our writing and in our environmentalist efforts, we have both felt the difficulty of preserving this connection. Knowing that the climate crisis has already begun to change the world, but not yet able to feel the full impact of those changes, we have sometimes found ourselves with little more than numbers to contend with: 1.5 degrees of warming or two; the voices of experts announcing in abstract terms what each might mean. The intangibility of the crisis has made it difficult to grapple with, in our actions as in our writing.

Turning to narratives grounded in nature has helped us to cross this distance, and *Channel* is born of the hope that such storytelling might do the same for others. We believe that poetry and prose can also provide a foundation for the bold imaginings necessary to face what changes this crisis demands of us.

In selecting work for Issue 1, we looked for writing which asked us to consider our natures as inseparable from the natural world, which fostered in us a deep empathy for other species, and which implored us to imagine and embrace the other. Nature writing as a genre is a longstanding and variously defined tradition. In *Channel* we have chosen to present nature writing of the sort we found we needed most—writing that frames nature as a foundation for thought and feeling and, in this time of crisis, might play a role in rebuilding connection in a dangerously fragmented world.

The devastation of our age is undeniable. And yet: "hope grows everywhere / like moss on the wall of a toilet" (D.S. Maolalai, *Channel*, 24); and yet "life / continues / dwindling on / the tilting earth" (Paul Lewis, *Channel*, 84).

Cassia Gaden Gilmartin and Elizabeth Murtough

John Paul Davies

Sea Swell

In the flesh of these wings
sea swells,

salt in their workings
salt in their sweat.

Rising in the marrow, rain
makes every cell mutinous as rivers.

Worked by salt these wings
wind, take me higher

to consider sea or sky
before I dry out,

before sun makes horizon,
makes sense of this greyness.

The wind will take me down and up
and only so far

before I nose
nerve-straight for the water,

gills squalling for breath;
before the current turns,

or whatever turns the current stops,
whatever moves me on strings of air,

whatever shakes out the sea
like a blanket in the backyard.

Joey Lew

As Alive

Good day sir / madam / do you have a second /
to talk about / yourself / I'm writing this article /
on sonder / just now / I want to confirm that you are /
so are you // why should I believe you // my grandfather
says that he is / as well / but he
is dead / which is another kind / of is / and I am
another kind / of asking / what particles make you
enough / what waves exchanged on pavement /
in grinning all 42 of those muscles / your nerves will
report / to your brain / but what if your brain
isn't // then what // my pup looks at me / this interview
strategy will not make me / new friends / his ears say /
but how else / how else to know if anybody else /
can see / every shade of green

Joey Lew

In My Backyard

the old oak tree knotted and stooped
is unevenly lilting in its
wind-howl at evening time,

supping softly on the air I've released.
Its boughs are bent toward my kitchen window,
its roots bursting out of the tomato patch.

Before its entrance—the garden bloomed
blustering red tomatoes but then—
in the center sprouted this unwanted

seed and I asked it to quietly re-root
in a space more convenient to my needs—
to cease this relentless overachievement—

but this tree has a vocation,
and will not leave. The tomatoes
may wilt, it's true. But it isn't the tree's fault.

The resources are scarce, and survival
is not a sin. My family too have left
patch after patch, so today,

the tree and I plant our feet and hand in branch
we sway in the tomato patch,
winds changing and buckling our knees.

Grace Wilentz

Belly of the Whale

After days
of not speaking to anyone
the sound of my voice
echoes back to me,
like the voice of a stranger.

Ribs come together above me
as church rafters.

Time is parceled out in the silences between
the slow-beating life of this beast,
the groan of its body,
the shrill song of its calls.

I remember watching it rise,
mountainous.
I considered its swooping frown and thought:
how very like a clown's mouth!
before it opened with a yawn
and the suck of water pulled me in like a riptide.

And then: silence, unlit dark.

Brief, but there are the moments when
I feel myself to be
in a darkened theatre.

Sometimes, I can feel us diving,
weightless, as I dream.

Rosamund Taylor

On the Lichens and Liverwort of Bantry Bay

1.

Sweat-stained,
  vomits beef-tea, eggs, milk;
twenty-six years old
  as life betrays her.
  White dust weighs Ellen's skull.

She loses all words to the work of illness:
work to find a bearable moment,
crumpled into the bed.

She once thought of herself as
    a bee
    a minnow.

2.

Then—
  then—

she comes back to her skin,
she can depend at last on mouth and breath and
stomach.

Cool linen sheets, a basin of hot water.
   Every moment glows—

   a paint brush, a wasp sting,
   mixed scent of seaweed
         and gorse.

3.

Flowers: colour first, then shape of petal.
Wild carrot, devil's-bit scabious, purple loosestrife,
self-heal.

Like a meal, four courses,
   Ellen was starving and finally, finally—

Bantry, drawn by honourable tug of tide. Pale, stooped
   she kneels in the landscape of old gods—
   foreshore, peninsula, stone, stream,
      turn of Earth, suck of bog.

First she presses flowers,
then she paints—
   a bog orchid, purple, green and green,
   liverwort,
      begins to use all her blues and yellows
   for shades of green and green in lichen.

4.

Light
   different on a boat, mountains luminous,
   bay low and huge. Wavelets suck away edges.
   Her hands silver
she finds the strength
   first to sit upright in the prow
   then to steer, row.

Silver nets
gathering kelp, seaweed—
coils without familiar names.
Ellen looks up salt-licked weeds in books,
words she repeats over and over:
   cladonia squamosa, lobaria virens

Liverwort, moss: like finding a litter of mice
in a drawer, pink, helpless, urea-sharp.
      their paws already clawed,
      eyes bulging behind pink skin,
      bands of milk showing
      through translucent stomachs—

pathetic, like her tiny plants,
which were nameless until she named them
yet thrived under the relentless sky.

5.

Rooks smashing crabs on Whiddy Island.

6.

All winter, painting, grey light weighs the windows.
All the hours of all the months disappear in her brush.

Ellen feels herself
    fading again. Slow to sit up,
the ache in her head, hard to think,
            to swallow—

She rests smouldering face against the glass.
In Bantry bay, red kelp opens for her.
      She feasts.

Note: Ellen Hutchins (1785-1815) was advised to take up botany while she convalesced from a long illness. Around Bantry Bay, she discovered numerous new species of moss, lichen and seaweed, and her paintings of specimens were widely respected.

Rosamund Taylor

No Natural Predators

Pangolin,
does your mother lick your pointed snout?
Do you smell of new leaves and milk?

In 1584, a fish climbed a tree.
A brown fish, long-tailed,
it erupted from the river Goa
and scuttled into leafy branches.
A most peculiar dog, said the Dutchman.

A panacea, the scales cure all illness,
cancers and fevers, infertility,
though she looks like a pinecone as she curls
to hide her tender stomach, her low dugs.
She wears her magic thin.

Pangolin,
do you taste the wind as you climb the canopy?
What sound do your feet make?

Elusive, hiding in red dust,
seeing one is like finding an asphodel
growing feathery flowers in the bog
and knowing it's also a plant of Elysium,
belonging only to gods.

The crystal methamphetamine dreams

of forests shining gold and silver,
red ants and long, sticky tongues.
Inhaled, a kilo of dusty scales
speeds the hit. A pinch of eternity.

Pangolin,
does the dry earth miss you? Or the rivers?
Did you dream of sticky tree-bark, of rain?

Jan Carson

Florence, Oregon

A cop is trying to shift everyone off the beach. "Get a move on fellas," he says. "Quickly now. It's not safe here."

He wears both thumbs hooked into his belt, arms forming handles against his torso. You look at the shape of him shadowed against the bright, winter sky and that teapot song from years ago comes scuttling into your head. *"Here's my handle. Here's my spout. Pick me up and pour me out."* You can't help yourself. You smile right up into the cop's big, flaccid face. He glares back. He looks as if he'd raise his foot and kick you if he could, the same way you'd lay into a mangey pup.

You're used to this. Men cannot abide you smiling. They don't even like you looking at them. You've practiced your smile a thousand times in the mirror. The barest slip of curled lip. Crinkled eyes. Just enough tooth to appear earnest. You can't see any difference between your mouth and the other fellas' folding up in mirth. But, most men seem to know. They don't want you near them or even looking. They do not want you brushing against them in the coffee line. The cop is squaring his chest and upping his voice now, angling his hipped gun so you can see he's packing heat. He's trying to look authoritative, like a cop he's seen on some television show. You think he looks daft, like a cartoon of himself.

Still, you'd swap places if you could. Just to stand as he is standing: legs spread, boots half-buried in the sand, shoulders raised as if to say, "I have every right to stand here on this beach."

Most people are ignoring the cop. They are taking photos.

Each flash flusters the seagulls who've settled close to the corpse. They rise suddenly, hover and seconds later return to earth like plastic bags caught in the circling breeze. People are shuffling slowly round the edge of it, handkerchiefs and coat sleeves held against their noses to muffle the stench; a putrid smell, like raw meat gone off. Some people are touching it. You watch them raise their hands and run a finger down its dark, grey belly. You imagine it is cold and slimy, but you could be wrong. You touched a snake once and couldn't believe how dry its skin was, closer in feel to fingernail than flesh.

"Touch it, Johnny," yells Frank.

He shoulder-barges you so you stumble in the sand. You only just avoid falling face first into it. You catch your vomit just before it leaves your mouth, swallow it down and smile as if you're having a great old time. All the other fellas are watching. They expect you to go after Frank now, to wrestle him down or pitch some choice words in his direction. Bastard. Wanker. Asshole. You don't. You can't. You know exactly how you should be, but your whole body is stiff. It will not bend to meet the moment.

Now the cop has found a megaphone. He is screeching at certain static individuals, threatening arrest and other unlikely consequences. It isn't what he says but the sheer shrill of him tinning against the Pacific wind which drives everyone off the beach. Into the sand dunes they go, seventy or so otherwise unrelated individuals, single file against the wind. They gather together in tight clusters about a quarter of a mile from the corpse. Families. Fishermen. Groups of young people raising their woolly shoulders for an extra inch of heat. Everyone's heard about the whale. Everyone's curious.

You stand with the other fellas, shivering in your sheepskin jacket, trying to keep the shake of yourself still. Frank is not shivering. Neither is Tom. Andy is not shivering, even though he's out in nothing but a plaid shirt. You wonder what it would feel like to put your arm around his checked shoulders and share your own small heat, the smoke and fresh sweat smell of him coming off on your jacket. Then tomorrow, when you wake, the same smell, diminished, but still present on your pillow. You wonder the same thing about Tom and Frank. You've no specific interest in any one of them, only the broad need to be warmer, to be not so always by yourself.

In the past you've tried with girls, hoping the press of flesh against stranger flesh would be enough to still your need. It has never been enough. You've found yourself on sofas and spare room beds with perfectly nice girls—Caroline, Melanie, two different kinds of Lorraine—and wondered how you arrived at this strange place. You've stroked and tongued, excavated various summer blouses, yet never once managed to be anything but absent, circling the farthest edge of yourself. This is my hand, you've thought, and it is cupped around a breast. This is my mouth, moving against another mouth. But, it is not your mouth or your hands, or even your eyes, looking. You don't know who is inside you, staring out.

The girls don't seem to notice. Or perhaps they do. You've seen the way they look down the side of your kissing face as if they are imagining someone else's tongue slugging around their mouth, someone else's cold hands, grasping. Afterwards, when you drive them home, they say, "Thank you. I had a lovely time," and close the car door gently like a dry cheek kiss. They are too polite to say anything honest. Or maybe they don't have the word for exactly how you are different from the other fellas. You think this word will be "gay" but you're not sure yet.

Sometimes you speak the shape of it, standing in front of the bathroom mirror. You watch your reflected self, noting the way your jaw shoots out and comes neatly back together. Your lips and your pale, yellow teeth. You have not yet let the sound of this word out. You haven't dared.

"Look," says Frank, raising his voice against the wind. "They're setting the dynamite."

He passes the binoculars round the group. You wait your turn. You are always last. If it is an activity requiring three participants, you will not even be included. By the time the binoculars get to you they are lukewarm from being handled. You press them against your eyes, relishing the extra blush of heat. At first you see only smudged black. Then your eyes adjust to the lens. You see sand dunes. Grey sky. Tom's face so close it is only a soft, peached blur. You pass your own hand in front of the lens. It is bloody pink and glowing slightly, like sliced meat held up to the light.

"I am full of blood," you think and the thought of all that warm redness swishing round your chest makes the air rush to your head. You are all of a sudden lighter than you should be. You think you might faint. There is nothing to lean on in a sand dune, nothing but grass and people, and you know they won't hold your weight.

You swallow the dizziness down and turn to face the beach, squinting through the sea grass as you pan the length of the corpse. You note its blunt nose and bloated belly. Its large Y-shaped tail and the swished hollow this tail has left in the sand. Without water you forget you are looking at a whale. It's only a heavy looking interruption in the sand: a kind of naturally occurring rock. You cannot imagine it light enough to float suddenly to the surface and spout. You can't imagine it swimming. You can tell it is dead, even from this distance. There is a difference between a thing which is not moving and a thing which cannot move.

The coastguards are gathering on the whale's northern side to dig holes and shove sticks of dynamite deep into the ground. They are hoping the explosion will solve the bulk of the problem, leaving the seagulls to deal with those small pieces of blubber which might linger afterwards. Earlier you heard the chief coastguard explain this to a news reporter, up from Portland to cover the story. The reporter's hands twitched at the word explosion, then quickly pocketed themselves. Professionalism, he was trying to say, with his sharply pressed slacks and tie, his good shoes now ruined by the sand. Professionalism, and something about being from a more sophisticated place. But you could tell his mouth was itching to shout "boom."

An older man asks to borrow the binoculars. You pass them to him, hand accidentally grazing gloved hand.

"I've seen whales beached before," he says, "but never a beast this size. They'll be lucky to shift the half of it tonight."

"Really, Sir?" you say. "Sure looks like a heck of a lot of dynamite to me."

"We'll see, son," he says and hands the binoculars back to you, smiling.

You smile back. Just a little smile. Closed lips. No teeth. The old man does not curl away. He doesn't even flinch. You wish there was a way to thank him for his kindness. You could offer a cigarette or a piece of gum. This would be entirely appropriate. This would not involve the crossing of a line. But you don't smoke and you've left your gum in the glove compartment, next to the maps. So you smile again—the same cautious lip twitch—and return to the other fellas. You can't risk stretching a good moment thin.

Everyone is watching the beach and the whale, which, any second now, will be consumed by a dreadful force.

All seventy of you are leaning forwards and also back, faces preceding heels by a good half foot. From above you must look like so many sheaves of corn, wind bent in one smooth direction. You are every single one, flinching. The flinch is a tightness in your shoulders, a dry click at the back of your throat, a constant stuttering blink caught in the fold of your eye like an unending loop of Morse code. Any second now there will be an explosion. And it isn't the bright flare of it you fear, or even the force of air rushing up the beach and into the dunes. It is the noise. The noise is a truth you have been all your life wanting and very much avoiding. You look at the men and occasional women grouped around you. You wonder if they are also afraid, if there are loud noises stuck in their throats too. If they sometimes need to roar. And can't.

Most of the bystanders are locals. It's too late in the season for holidaymakers though a few curious individuals have driven from the next town over just so they can say they were here. You imagine them, weeks from now, whiskey tumblers in hand, recounting the incident at dinner parties and corporate mixers. "Magnificent creature," they'll say. "It's a shame to see it come to such a sorry end." You cannot imagine yourself there, next to them, laughing in a suit. Even years from now, when you will have reached the age of thirty or forty. You cannot picture yourself anything but awkward, standing in a corner by the drinks table, spearing olives and insipid cheddar cubes, feeling your hands turn clammy against your glass.

Then the whale explodes.

At first there is no noise. The sand goes feathering up in a wide fountain. The shape of this is a kind of soft, inverted pyramid. A cloud of smoke envelops the sky, blood red and blond where the beach has come away with the whale. You can't see through this cloud to the ocean beyond. You can't see whether the corpse is still present or 3, 2, 1 vanished like some mad magician's trick. You can't keep from staring, marvelling at the silence and the bloody colours, the way the dynamite has turned the entire beach into a canvas, the shocked seagulls rising en masse like individual rain drops returning to the clouds.

Then the noise catches up with you.

A dull thud which lands in your ears and also the pit of your stomach. Which drives your heels deeper into the sand and thunders through your groin, bidding every part of your body retreat. You look at the other fellas. Tom is covering his ears. Frank is also covering his. Andy has toppled backwards into the sea grass. The white soles of his sneakers hover just above the sand like a pair of speech marks, cupping their own surprise. Andy is trying to cover his ears. His hands scrabble round his head as if they have forgotten where an ear should be and what it should feel like when touched. His face is without any kind of expression. Not even shock. All the people standing round you are blank as unspoilt paper. You wonder if your own face is also empty. You lift a hand to your mouth, feel the parched stiffness of your lower lip, bitten by the wind, the way your jaw is hanging open like a trap. You close your mouth.

Then the blood begins to fall.

Not just blood but flesh also, and long, slathering sections of intestine still wet from the whale's inside. Propelled by momentum, the heaviest sections drop first. They fall from the sky like a shower of lost meteorites: fist-sized hunks and bloody lumps, some as big as a child's head. One, then two, then seven, eight, nine, two dozen blubbered chunks slamming into the sand so hard they leave craters. Clud. Clud. Clud. Each impact makes a wet thud. People jump at the first cludded impact. They turn to catch the second. After three, they begin to bolt towards the car park and the road beyond. They roof their arms above their heads as if they are being attacked from above. Their feet will not take them straight. In and out of the sea grass they go like creatures crazing in the headlights.

You do not move. The whale parts drop all around you. It is like you are standing in the middle of the meat counter at Fred Meyer's. A tooth-coloured fragment of bone—rib most likely—spears itself into the sand, just a half foot from your toe. You don't want to look at it directly, but you don't move away either. In the distance you hear the first windscreen shatter under impact. Just behind you and to the left a girl begins to scream and doesn't stop. The noise comes out of her in short, breathless pants. The other fellas have all bolted but you don't move. You don't think about moving. You don't think about not moving either. You just stand there, looking up at the sky, waiting for the end of it all.

Then the blood really begins to fall.

A plague of it. A cloud of bloody spit. It skips the dunes and goes soaring past at low cloud level. You hear it hissing overhead. It goes *spsssssss* as it passes as if it is a host of tiny insects, swarming. You could raise a hand and catch it if you wanted. One arm. One hand. You could come away red. Marked by this moment as everyone else will be marked. It wouldn't take much, only a slight movement on your part. But you don't. You can't. Your whole body is stuck. And then it is too late. The blood has passed you by. It is too late to say, "Look at me, covered in little bits of exploded whale. Look at me, just the same as all the other fellas."

All the other fellas are waiting for you in the car park. They are red. They are dripping. They are swiping at their wet faces with balled up Kleenex, only moving the blood from one bit of skin to another, leaving slick marks on their skin like brush strokes lining in paint. Andy runs his hand through the front of his hair. His hand comes away red. His hair stays up in a smooth wave. Soon it will begin to crust. You imagine him later in the shower, shampooing and rinsing and repeating the cycle three or four times at least. Not feeling entirely clean. You only let yourself imagine his naked feet, the black hairs curling on each toe, the pinkish water, like raspberry Kool Aid, swirling round the plughole.

"Jesus," he says, his teeth chitter-chattering so fast you can barely make the words out. "What the Hell just happened?"

"Whale," says Tom, almost choking on his own voice.

"Boom," says Johnny, throwing his arms up like a Southern Baptist.

"Jesus," says Tom. And then they are all at the same time laughing and falling over and trying to roll each other into the bloody puddles in a way that says I will cry about this later, when there's no one there to see.

"The whale's still there," you say. "The dynamite didn't work. Most of it didn't explode."

But the other fellas aren't listening. And the car park is full of other bloody people who are not listening. They are wiping at themselves with picnic rugs, rubbing the worst of it off in the sand. They are placing carrier bags on car seats so the upholstery won't be ruined. They are already wondering how they will tell this story to their wives and their children. They are not noticing you, on the edge of the car park, so white, so clean it is like you have never been touched.

D.S. Maolalai

Crabs and Netted Mackerel

we rolled boats
homeward; birds
calling after
and the corners
of the world
turning surfaced
like the inside
of a bowl
filled with cherries.

somewhere
people
were buying drinks
on beaches
and old men
were looking to waves. somewhere
we were to be welcomed
like heroes. our load
was crabs,
lobsters
and netted mackerel. veg
would be peeled when we got in,
roasted apples
and opened wines.
the best drunks in town
would already be steaming.

hope grows everywhere
like moss on the wall of a toilet.
love was coming.
great
and stinking love.
the boats rocked
with anticipation,
gentle
as the parts of a clock.

when storms come
they come suddenly
and always from behind us
and we are lost
within distance of the pier.

D.S. Maolalai

Dandelion Clocks

I explore tradition
for her amusement. the old one;
where you blow
until all the seeds are gone
to tell what time
it is. and the new ones,
fresh
from primary school—
how if you touch the juice
from the stem
you'll piss yourself. and using them
to show
who likes butter. strange, the lessons
which grow up
around plants. strange too, explaining it too,
after having to tell someone
that the yellow ones
are the white ones
but in different stages
of season.

Martina Dalton

The Actual Stag

These are not my eyes
I cannot see.
This is not my voice
I cannot speak.

My mouth, carved
From a solid piece of wood
Cannot shut.
Dribbles air like milk.

My coat is wet with sog
It trips me.
The compass in my soul
Takes me

Leads me on
Till I am lost
All over in this very place
Where I was born.

A chord wrapped around
My voice
Is pulled—released, then pulled.
It wears me out.

A pair of trees have sprouted
Just above my eyes.
I am so tired of carrying
This trophy on my head.

I cannot put it down
Or find
That missing thing.
I don't know what it looks like.

Elspeth Wilson

We cannot eat hares

"We cannot eat hares because they are beautiful," you tell me
but I already know that beautiful things get eaten

like my body in bite-sized chunks before it's time,
a butterfly floating before a dog,
a clashing of animal parts beneath sheets.

"Hares enchant us, they are of the earth and fairy tales,"
you say, dividing flesh from flesh
with knife and mind,
decreeing one sinew morsel and another deity.

We cannot eat hares.
They are beautiful, I know this much.

Colin Hopkirk

Buzzard

Walking out of the valley
after a morning of searching,
sun-squinted, I find her
wheeling away,
sailing
high and
slow
and far,
distancing herself,
then turning
and, slowly
returning
until,
circling overhead,
she stares me down.
In an instant
I am re-natured,
astounded,
my heart in her heart
my eye in her eye.

John Creevy

In the Garden

See the plane slice the sky; the ozone-blue sundered by jet-trails. He wants to grasp them, to twine his fingers through the clouds and pull the whole thing down. It will crush him, press him into the ground where the two of them once dug with pilfered kitchen spoons. He can see it now, the sterling silver in his brother's hand and the rocks that hide clambering insects. *They're gonna crawl into you. They're gonna lay eggs in that broken fucking brain of yours and…* Stop. Breathe. Count the magpies. There are seven of them, but he can't remember the rhyme. He hopes it means good luck. He hopes Darren will understand why he had to come here, why he had to sign himself out. He knows they're looking for him. The old house is the only thing they haven't touched yet. Chipped pink paint and a chimney choked by ivy. It lies beyond their white gloves, their poison pills. They must have found his things by now, the wallet and mobile he left outside his brother's house. Darren is probably yelling at someone over the telephone. He will wait here for him in the garden. He will watch the evening wheeze to a close as he grips the grass around him, holding close as he can to the ground.

Patrick Deeley

Begun Things

Clay on your skin and under your nails, clay
in your eyes and ears, clay tongue
and teeth, clay-tonsilled throat, oesophageal clay,
clay heart, belly bowl of clay—why,
she laughs, maybe even clay feet, the famous

actress old and careless what anyone thinks,
whose name has slipped your mind
and whom you are unsure how to face:
a handshake, a nod, an air kiss? Clay
compliments for your marl make-up, mascara

and lipstick part of her personal clay,
hoarse voice consumptive of nicotine, frailty
crowned with flaxen coiffure, spendthrift
rootless lips, no rest in her flickering fingertips;
yet she waits, her sapphire stare

requiring more than a shrug or foot-shift,
and it's not as if the tribute she extends, singing
the streams and dams of your lingo,
the way they snorkel and spill
into the ecosystem of a poem, plumb

the pleasure-give of ditches, potential of rifts,
sumps, undipsticked quag catches,
world as it was and will be again, is duty-bound,

or that her avowal of how absent
you grow to yourself—mirrored in a pool

of thought, tilting a ladle of words, tasting
silt pottage with only the press
of the wind filling your ear, only the close
iridescence of sticklebacks arrowing—is routine
or that she suggests your song

will lead to success or contentment;
it's not loneliness unless her sashay, waited on
hand and foot, is loneliness; then,
too late, as she smiles, turns to leave, you know
it's the allure of begun things, urge

to meld the primal with the modern, even
to where will-o'-the-wisp is glimpsed
hovering next a streetlamp while from the stone
fountain in the square a behemoth
spouts as it breaks the surface of the waterland.

Amanda Bell

Dodder River Haiku

narrow hill road
a short-horned cow
glowers from the ditch

reservoir spillway
the scent of elderflower
on a warm breeze

stopping for a snack
beneath the draping larch
a cloud of midges

urban river path
gulls and two plump foxes
eating sandwiches

Dodder Valley walk
two sheep and a lamb
tending the lawn

a baby rat disappears
down the heron's throat—
camera shutters snap

beneath the ring road
a 'Men at Work' sign floating
past the heron

warm summer evening
sharing a picnic on the weir
two grey crows

lone fox on the bank
onlookers whisper
about poisoned cubs

Lucy Crispin

January sends a short but important memo

We climb slowly along the winter valley's side,
cold enough to welcome the blood thud of walking,
warmed, too, by the rhythm of talk and no talking
which good friends have. Communion-hunger satisfied,
the self re-orients, in centripetal
motion. We turn at the track's end by the old hall
to see a twin black sleekness of birds, distant-small:
two cormorants at the mere's edge, where skeletal
trees, coppiced into base-bunched clumps, are precisely
mirrored in the cloud-bright water. A coot leaves—
opened by the soft prow of its breast as it cleaves
the surface—a single, perfect, widening vee
of wake. Paused, we notice how the wall's moss glows
with the light it gathers; how deep the silent air goes.

Ojo Taiye

at the age of four

it's July and i am tired
the sun refused to burn
through the gauze of cloud

i am living a life that once
existed only in my mother's dream
i cradle the bodies from a war

a child made from bullets
& powdered milk
the dead stay dead

    a lone starling wheels & drops
    on a powerline close
    to my window

    & what i know grows dim
    like what absence means
    my mouth a technology

    of softness
    a kite i refuse to pull
    down from the sky

        the sharp oak fingers
        of faith refusing

to abandon me

what use is an unfinished form
when all i want is to open up
& unreel

what use
days to come will crack
open without her image

the stars fading
the streetlight becoming
her arms around my body

distance is a kind of quantum
bond like an attachment to the cold
snow in her lungs

what i mean is i learned
& the night creaks of branches
& i stand listening

Suzzanna Matthews

Hope Arise

We spent our summers back east, remember us little sister, catching fireflies at night, counting stars. Recall the strangeness of cricket song
In the dark we shared stories, pondered out our *wonder whys…*

There were firsts, first climbed trees, first kissed boys, and other try, tried, tries
By the water we called out for everything, for all that we could ever long
And father said, she'd soon be home, gave us hope akin to lies

He gave us this, a spell, to count the miles between thunder and lightning skies
But how do we keep safe from the hum of the heart, the Pacific, the Atlantic pounding throng
in all those raged storms?

All between they were drawn, boundaries, down the shores, all those lines
Home, out West our eyes, hair too dark. Back East our skin too light, always wrong,
Despite so many cousins, uncles, aunts, so much history, so many ties

East, West, East, West, our breathe calm then, we run,

deer-leap, high
over that unseen abyss. When she was with us we never stumbled,
There was comfort in what we could not know would falter

We realized too young, too acutely, that the most fervid deep green summer dies,
learned to hold through storms, to hold fierce among tearing wreckage,
Holding hands, gripping arms, near fused together, becoming one, no yous no Is
Like our skicin ancestors, we danced around fire, our feet in flames,
Our loss ever burning, we conjured hope, like smoke—arise

"Skicin" is one of several Passamaquoddy words to refer to ancestors. Pronounced "skee-jin," the word refers to people whose roots go back before the influx of Europeans.

Polly Waterfield

Bones

God guard me from those thoughts men think
In the mind alone;
He who sings a lasting song
Thinks in a marrow-bone.

W.B.Yeats, from 'A Prayer for Old Age'

What the bones know

I am trying to figure out what I know in my bones. I want to tell my story in order to understand how things are, to stand on my two feet in my own story. The gaps frighten me. There is before and after Extinction Rebellion, but what does this mean?

I know in my bones that at the heart of everything is interdependence. I know this through loss: I never had much tribe or the pleasure of enjoying and being enjoyed. I am learning about belonging but it's a cobbled-together jigsaw, not in my bones. Oh, to relax into being a small part of something bigger, something together. The sometimes suspect seductiveness of tribe.

Tribe

I am not a joiner but I long to belong. People hold hands around a cabbage patch and I give up a successful career to go and live with them. There are things that have eluded me: physical vitality, marriage, children. Some losses are more painful than others. People with families have tribe but I float between groups—this has its own freedom and purposefulness but there is no one to snuggle up to on a dark night. Where will I belong if things fall apart?

On the other hand, a group of us create gold and sea-green slow-sewn banners for our choir concerts. Oh! Creativity doesn't have to be solitary. A friend asks to hear my XR story and my voice pours out of me onto this page—shared thinking is a river I can swim in.

The well-worn pebble in my pocket reminds me of a timeless day at the beach and that every fragment of carefree companionship is radical, two people surviving each other and thriving.

Breakdown

I am newly arrived in the world—where are the others to help me make sense of this too-loud, too-big place? I am a child as thin as bones of time and I love oak apples, climbing the Fireworks Tree, peeping out at golfers from my hiding place. I *am* the landscape while I am in it. I am a gawky teenager in ochre corduroy shorts and I busy myself being clever and passing exams, but remember not a note of the Mozart violin concerto I've just played with the school orchestra, because of the terror.

I am a young adult. I am performing on stages around the world but all I can think about is will I drop my instrument. I must be happy because I am "successful." I crash and burn and escape to another country. I am successful again, and again fall apart and leave. Colourful motley musicians surround me but there is no one to hold me in mind as I crash and burn, crash and burn.

Closer to now, there are seventy people sitting around on

straw bales covered with worn velvet curtains, grappling together with how to be in these bleak times. Waves of despair and desire and dreaming move through the group like a natural force but some people need to close the door tight against the grimness. I walk to the centre, take the talking stick and speak, to honour those who are letting themselves break down.

I wish I could fall apart more deeply, lose my bones.

Mind the gap!

We know we have to mind the gap but this gap is everywhere and so huge no one notices it anymore. Climate breakdown is a reality but "Do you believe in climate change?" a young man casually asks his grandparents in a café, as though we can choose. I do my daily walk through the cool woods to Byron's Pool with the trees growing and all the birds jabbering and the river flowing as though there's nothing wrong. Between my experience and the horrifying headlines yawns an unspeakable space. I know the polar ice caps are melting and the Arctic peat is burning but I don't feel it in my bones. How can I mind this gap?

XR for introverts

I am "introvert." I am also now "activist." I used to be afraid of activists, glancing at them furtively out the corners of my eyes. I felt guilty by default, needing to justify the interiority of my life. What moved in them that didn't in me? Did it mean I didn't care if I wasn't taking action in that way?

I believe in inner work and increasingly in the power of collective thought. I don't want to think that all my years spent not on the streets were a waste and so I have to believe there are many ways of taking action, including some that look like inaction. I gave up a successful career and that signals offbeat priorities. "Why not re-train as a lawyer and use your gifts?" ask the well-meaning American relatives, not seeing I am broken. Instead I join with others in meditation and daily life to anchor something in the sand-dunes. I have the utmost respect for the Benedictine monks in a fold of the Scottish hills who "only" pray.

Now I am being simultaneously teased outwards and inwards. Will the centre hold?

Mother

My mother holds herself as though she has no bones to support her. She doesn't have a story. I know hardly anything of her family, of what has made her, her likes and dislikes. I know she is clever at the cryptic crossword puzzles and thinks anyone who hasn't read all of Jane Austen isn't up to much. She has made a sacrifice of her life—for my sake? She doesn't hear who I am, what my story might be. Maybe if I try harder to do better, to be better, to arrange myself around her, then she will hear me...

We call the earth our mother but I wonder if she is hearing us now as we scrabble to make sense of what is happening. Let's try harder, harder, harder... But perhaps she is deaf and cold, turning away her broad shoulder and deciding we don't have a story worth listening to anymore. Going on without us.

Enough

"But it isn't enough!" rings out the desperate response to some hopeful micro-initiative to do with goat husbandry. The speaker knows and values her despair and I understand it is her fuel for action and think I need to feel my despair more deeply. But it isn't enough for what? To save the planet, to save humankind—these are too big to weigh our actions against and in any case some people think it is too late. I respect the people who, with open eyes, are purposefully enjoying what can be enjoyed, moment by moment.

I am not enough to please my parents; I need to try harder, harder, harder... I am not enough to stand on stage and tell my story. I am not enough to keep up with the XR social media circus and because I am not volunteering for the million things that are crying out to be done. I am a hungry ghost and nothing is enough; I am condemned to feel famished the more I eat and I will consume everything around me until all that's left is bones.

I don't know what is enough in these times.

Moments of inexplicable happiness

My voice was never heard. By now in my sixties I have put together a patchwork of skills to help myself through but what comes out is unreliable, frustrating and often still not heard. At a Non-Violent Direct Action training day I am astonished to find myself speaking spontaneously and hearing an echo—others stand up in solidarity. My heart stands up too in the knowledge that there are people out there.

My first XR small group meeting: I announce myself with "I'm really not sure I want to be here," and it is accepted without question. Again: "I'm afraid I'm a rubbish rebel," and a young man welcomes me as part of the biodiversity we need not only in the world but in our group. My heart is touched.

In April, with friends, I step into the road at Marble Arch to block the traffic. Later I am at Oxford Circus with the pink boat. I am finding my way. I know how to notice who in the crowd is alone or out of the loop and speak to them. Rare inexplicable happiness rises up in me.

I am at Piccadilly Circus with the traffic all snarled up and a movingly small group of teenagers with truth in their eyes are holding the fort. I am terrified of conflict but I look at a stalled taxi and suddenly think "I can do this!" I cross the road, knock on the window and say "This must be really frustrating for you." The world doesn't end and energy streams through my bones and my whole body.

Passion

My passion is the potential of people: the sparkle in the young boy's eye after telling his XR story to more people than he's ever spoken to in his life, the long-honed skills of body or mind or both. This has been the ground bass to my life, the ocean floor beneath the waves, the one constant. A strange and lonely marriage to what might be possible.

In April I find myself on the streets of London along with many other impassioned people. That same evening another kind of Passion at King's College Cambridge: that of St Matthew. We are so close we breathe with the musicians in the story's wailing sorrow, and I feel connected to every one of my brilliant and heartbreakingly young men in the choir. "There will always be music," says my friend who knows how everything is tottering and is at peace with a terminal diagnosis for humankind. But not music like this; this is the pinnacle and pinnacles fall first. I am filled with a terrible sadness at the skill and the beauty and the passion of centuries and at how everything passes. I think I do not want to live in a world without Bach.

Can you hear me?

Childhood. Everything is lovely—we have all we need, our parents are glamorous, we live abroad and have our own typewriters. The children are clever and talented. How could there be anything wrong? I want a grown-up to tell me how bad things are. Surely it must be bad because of the monsters lurking in the gaps between people. But since no adult is paying any attention it can't really be wrong. Or someone would notice my mother's unhappiness. Or someone would ask me how I feel. Or someone would take my hand and introduce me to the world and help me find my story.

And now how bad are things? Can anyone hear me? Is the microphone working?

This is an emergency

It has always been an emergency. My mother has always been quietly dying; my parents have always been silently at war with each other; the baby has always been caught in the crossfire; there has never been enough attention to go around; it has always been clear that only one person can survive a relationship; other people have always been a threat. I know emergency; it is in my bones and blood and nervous system and now shows up in my blood pressure despite all the measures I've taken and all the help I've had.

So much for my personal emergency. Is it so different from what is destroying life on earth? I wonder if it's possible for humankind to thrive along with the earth but I fear my imagination is limited to only one survivor and that's obviously not us.

We are all dying all the time and there is more dying at stake now, but civilisations do rise and fall. We are falling, most likely.

Heartbroken

Some wisdom for troubled times came my way: find the thing that breaks your heart and then plough your energy into that. What breaks my heart is my mother's life, the wasteland of her marriage, the way she dwindled and died not so old, unspeakably alone. What breaks my heart is the pain passed down through generations because another way couldn't be found, the unspeakable couldn't be spoken. What breaks my heart is how the pain lodges in bones and tissues and is passed on again and again.

If you need a signpost here is another: you do not have to comprehend or control everything, but to learn which story you are in and which of the many things calling out in the world is calling to you. My story is something to do with the body, with myself as a creature of the earth. My story is to grapple with this every day.

I help someone align her bones, her mind and her movement and she sheds a suit of armour, gracefully and gratefully. The tears fall. This is my work, to arrive in my body on the earth and to know it as home.

What breaks your heart?

Two things

My sister-in-law is upstairs in the spacious German farmhouse where they have taken refuge, in agony from the brain tumour which will end her life at thirty-three. I can't find my way through all this pain. But there are also the huge jugs of chamomile tea in the comforting kitchen and the quiet presence of people who work the land and know the pressure of bringing in the harvest when the earth is so generously abundant. They are adults—not the kind who aren't listening—and they know something that I don't. Frau Kugel sits with my sister-in-law in pain and something passes between their bodies.

There is the agony and the unbearableness and there is also something else. I want to know the something else.

We don't know

Does the world need an engineer more than a singer in these times? In all obvious ways, yes—but surely it isn't as simple as that.

My classical singer friend who just died, inexplicably and no older than me, imagined himself as a storyteller on the road with his harp in the dark days to come. A travelling healing minstrel for ragged times with his big and beautiful voice. Then, in our twenties, I was scared by his vision but now I honour him by remembering what he never became.

This can't be fixed. This is bigger than any of us. I don't think anyone can know what the world needs.

Too big, too small

I am close to the ground and clutching my mother's thumb, small and sheltered underneath the umbrella of her skirts. I feel secure. Older, I am outside with the family in the warm dark night of the Indian subcontinent, supposedly relaxing after a meal brought by the bearer whom my father has treated with his usual condescending bonhomie. I look up at the stars and suddenly disappear into the too-bigness—I can't breathe, can't think, can't speak. I am too small; the world is too big. My blood and bones are turned to stone and there's no one to bring me back to life.

Later I escape from my successful life and find refuge

elsewhere. “World service” and “transformation of consciousness” are terms too big for me, but all the same it’s the first place I feel at home. I unfurl a little, find my bones a bit. It takes all my strength to keep unfurling as life rolls on and I move on, and maybe this is selfish. I create my life.

“Affairs are now soul-sized,” and mostly I am too small and the things I am trying to think about too big. With a friend I remember that it’s still okay to have everyday concerns, and I can breathe again. But where are the big conversations? Maybe everyone feels too small.

Tell the truth!

I live with a dead mother though my mother died long years ago. Every day I work to revive her and this is hard work but necessary.

I am fifteen: a letter from my brother shatters the illusion of “everything is fine” and tells the truth about our mother’s unhappiness, exploding my world with terror and with hope. So I know in my bones that life bursts forth when the elephant is named.

I smile at the elephant at Marble Arch saying “Ecocide” and celebrate with the pink boat at Oxford Circus saying “Tell the truth!”

Yours in love and rage

Love, yes, but what about rage? It’s still a bit of a shock seeing this at the end of many XR missives. I respect people’s outrage especially young people’s but I’m hoping it won’t be directed at me. Anger frightens me. I wish I could ‘rage, rage against the dying of the light,’ but my rage is buried too deep to be summoned at will. All the same, something has got me willing to go on the streets and maybe it isn't just the love and hugs.

Dreaming

My father says pityingly "Pol... you and your dreams..." No place for dreams or dreamers in the world of "his" war. I only ever wanted to breathe freely, to move easily, to belong. Now I am older and stiffer and the air is full of invisible particles but I am still dreaming.

I am half-buried in the ground. I can't move; the sun bears down on me. My sisters are being taken to the knackers – they are still beautiful but they are old and are not considered of value. Around me are other horses also buried. We can't move our legs though it's our joy and delight to move and to run over the earth. This goes on for a few centuries.

Now my legs are above ground; I am ably supported upside down at the sacrum, the sacred bone, and I am an ice skater. I have found my life partner! Torvill and Dean! Delightedly performing wild, erotic gymastic moves in the air with my upside down legs. This is in public and I know this changes everything.

I don't have a daughter but she is dead by the roadside, her vulnerable knees showing through raggedy black jeans. I cycle on through the summer hedgerows, not wanting to know. In any case I haven't had a daughter. I don't know if it was a violent death but something tells me it was. Can something die that hasn't even existed? How can I mourn for something I didn't know I had?

In my bones, I know that I have to tell my tribe. I tell them. It is received. I am overwhelmed with grief.

Habitat

There is no Planet B, as the placards and the book tell us.

Planet A is our home and so is the habitat of our bodies, the only chance we get. In my Alexander teaching work I wonder if there is a connection between the difficulty of listening to our fragile bodies and our blindness to the fragility of the earth. Maybe that connection means realising we will die and return to earth, return to being part of something. My desire is to know myself as habitat and part of the cycle of all things. I do what I can to help people restore their mind-body ecosystem, allow some territory for their own rewilding, reckon with the force of gravity in their bones, let themselves be supported by the earth and be part of what surrounds them. But not all want to listen.

I don't usually do this sort of thing

I really don't. I am not a natural-born rebel and find it hard to stand up to authority. But now there are a lot of people out there who also don't and aren't and this is wonderful. The issues aren't new; I am not new to the issues though perhaps I had gotten a bit sloppy in my choices. So why do I now want to shout jubilantly about Extinction Rebellion? Could it be there is enough of me in my muscles and tissues now to want to put my body there, on the streets? Or perhaps it's that I feel buoyed up by the tidal wave of the youth of the world at my back. For now, this seems to be my caravan. It seems these are my people, young and old. I can feel something different in my bones and I want to play my part. Together.

'Deep in our bones resides an ancient, singing couple who just won't give up making their beautiful, wild noise. The world won't end if we can find them.'

Martín Prechtel, from ' Secrets of the Talking Jaguar'

Karen O'Connor

Field of Gulls

Today I passed a field of seagulls,
planted, neat rows, like a field of cotton,
low to the ground, a sign of something.
White, the colour of purity,
today has a minatory feel,
the way they line up so still and rigid
their roots growing down into the sodden earth
their beaks reaching upwards, looking to the sky.

Today I passed a field of seagulls,
the same field as yesterday,
no different to the field before, or the one after,
except this field grows gulls by the kilo,
ready for harvesting,
to feed the cows into the dark,
hear their bellow in the fading light,
their exhale clouding the evening,
white feathers floating upwards to a bird-less sky.

Lisa Stice

Incidental

for Sagawa Chika

A cicada left its hollow husk on the fence post, and so
I made myself small to crawl inside but I had no wings.
In my appearance of desiccation, no bird or lizard wanted me.
What was there to do
but make my way to the garden
where I sloughed that borrowed skin beneath the sage.
I am larger now, my exterior soft.

Sagawa Chika (1911-1936; Japan): poet and translator

Lola Scollard

Life, Still with Pheasant

after Monet

For a whole week you didn't show.
We thought the neighbour had got you,
shot you,
imagined your head, lying
limp over the edge of his bare table,
him plucking you, gutting you, stuffing you,
roasting, basting, tasting you,
savouring you,
downing and drowning you
with a fine claret.

Then I saw it,
your red eye, cheery,
green hood, velvety,
white collar, gentlemanly,
bronze breast, speckled,
copper wings, polished,
long tail, striped:
our live Christmas decoration,
prince among birds,
sharing oat flakes,
bread-crumbs, apples,
tomatoes, rum
raisin and walnut cake
with robins, blackbirds,
wagtails and finches.

We didn’t offer turkey.

Iain Twiddy

Shannon

No late-breaking sun
to ease the day's passing;
just the midland mudlands in bloom—

skewed shelvings like petals
still milking the clouds,
months under the occupation of rain—

and the strew of cows' tongues
that must surely be tickling,
lapping up the March murk,

given this bloaty, breachy,
slippery, sloppy,
widening smile of a river.

Lydia Unsworth

Nothing that Understands Stays Silent

We ate the caterpillars. We looked at the live ones squirming in front of us, on a plate, on a leaf. Thought about finding it repulsive. But then the close-ups came, and I'm alright with eating anything that looks beautiful.

Transparency: A lake. A crack. A seam.

Buffaloes in charge

of the universe. Your legs,

amazing. Dwellings replete

with verse,

with chorus.

Tinny undertows of potential music. Gainfully, you undid what you gave. Gave it back, pretended that it never.

Remembering is a form of attention. Panic is a form of contemp-
lation. A tavern, a tabernacle, a boat, a carcass.

row me / row with me / row for me

The giant hunk of elegant belly flopped into the centre of the sort of sports hall, through the flood turned water turned floor turned lack of space. Sometimes it is enough simply to see. My insides. What wonder. Exhaust.

Foraging is a form of trying to be complete.

Lydia Unsworth

Chestnuts

Rocks in my moss for hundreds of years. Best place for them. Grass, and its tight little roots. A nail pulled out of a finger, a cut fringe allowed to drop into a bowl of food.

The soft underbelly of where things were

—absence pure as when a concave chestnut grows again against a convex chestnut and those two halves are pulled apart. Have you ever put your finger on that gap? It's the smoothest grain. The quantifiable difference between the thickness of a photo album and the place that life is. A face staring out from under an umbrella underneath the rain.

There's no time to remember. Maudlin ornaments harbour trauma. *Where were we?*

Where we were.

The straight road the dark night the tight light in my face and the kind arm shoving me through all the way. Grumpy and honest. Symbiotic levels of okay. The circumference of the hollow of a cave. Small bodies climb onto bigger bodies. Moss in our rocks, our bodies as rocks. Moss warms old shoulders, lower backs, growing outward from around the navel. The water calm today. Glass like glass. To glass. To be glassed. The sound of a material.

When carrying a coffin. Setting it down. We just want to be together, small clumps of together. The animals go in two by two. Hooray, we have fur to cling to. Rollercoasters make for fine ancestral mothers. Giants that we might once again be in arms.

David Butler

Annaghmakerrig

I

Returning after fifteen years
in a lean, cold season—the ground
numb from winter's pummelling.
A year of uncertainties. Even
in this retreat the spring has stalled:
nothing in leaf, but the promise of leaves;
a skittish wind scattering light
over the bright slate of the lake.

II

The House does its bit to hold time,
as Art aspires: the Cluedo floorplan;
the stone-flagged hall and wooden hue
of the various Dutch interiors.
Chancing into the Music Room,
an open score on the harpsicord
sets clefs and quavers prancing
like the prows of waiting gondolas.

III

What you hear, here, are silences:
the harp and piano, mute;
the volumes on antique shelves;
the corridors of oils;
the interrogative past
weighing on every floorboard.

What is it it asks of you,
of your half-a-lifetime?

IV

Each tree declares its certainty:
the Scots pine, the copper beech.
The woods resound with woodwind
of liveried birds. In the bull-rushes
a glissade of landing ducks,
whilst a woodpigeon, dusk-toned,
erupts on a high parabola. What
do *you* do? What do *you* do?

Don Ó Donnacháin

Derry 2084: A Burial

Jean thought she'd seen his face in the crowd. It wasn't him. She cursed under her breath.

All over the Old City, people were out enjoying the last of the sun or buying what they needed before the weather turned. There was a growing urgency about the place. Jean turned a corner, continuing the fine-tooth motions of combing the city for her son.

She hated anxiety in the sunshine.

It was still fine in Derry but heavy rains out across Donegal in past days had made for another Code Orange. When the Flash Flood Text Alert came in that morning, Jean sighed with annoyance. She turned to Ivor, who was crouched over his jar of tadpoles, and told him he couldn't wander today. He'd have to stay near.

No answer.

"Did you hear me, love?"

"Uh-huh."

His eyes were so close to the jar opening that Jean could only see his back and shoulders—a curious decapitation framed by the window of northern springtime light.

The nurses had said Ivor's growing detachment was a classic sign of early puberty. Up until not very long ago—perhaps just a few months back—Jean could barely shake him off.

For much of his infancy, Ivor followed her around, even in the house, ensuring there was some form of contact between them at most times. If contact was refused or not possible when he needed it, he could get nervous and upset. Sometimes, his distress would escalate into hysterics—inconsolable, tearful howls followed by rounds of airless convulsions, or more violent outbursts when he cursed his mother and looked about for things of hers to fling or break.

When this happened, Jean would have to get hold of him somehow and envelope him with her body, restraining his wriggles and kicks, and exaggerate her breathing so that his own would gradually slow down and synchronise with hers. Once, during this de-escalating process, blood from a cut she'd gotten on her forehead, from broken glass he'd thrown at her, trickled into her eye. A sharp sting hit. She shut her eyes tightly. The blood collecting on her scrunched-up eyelid began to drip onto Ivor's cheek below and a thought briefly passed through Jean that if she held him long enough, or a little tighter, the breathing might slow so much that it would stop altogether and that might be best for everyone.

What followed such episodes was a most unique kind of peace—love found again in the aftermath of violence. These were the most tender moments of Jean's life.

By the time Ivor started school—he didn't go till he was six—there were dramatics every morning at the school gates where he clung tightly to her legs, screaming, and bit or spat if she tried to pry him away. It was as if he had split her in half, directing all his love and need to her legs and all his hate and fear to her arms and face.

Jean ended up having to sit in with him for the first half hour or so of every school day, until he got engrossed by patterns in the sand box or a structure he was trying to make out of the wooden blocks. She would then steal away. With time, Ivor learned to make the daily switch of his attachment from Jean to Mrs. Moon, his P1 teacher. Each year brought a new teacher and a new attachment. As he grew, the cast of trusted attachees expanded, so that, by the time he was ten, Derry intramuros was like a playground for him. He'd wander off, run up to people he knew well. He could spend hours walking the Walls on his own, studying, as he moved, the changing lines and angles of the Old City below.

And yet, whenever they'd venture outside the City Walls—to visit friends up in Irish Town or do the weekly shop at the Waterside Complex—his hand would soon find its way into his mother's and clasp it tightly, his step would fall in with hers and before long, he'd be walking so close to her that, on a few occasions, he caused her to stumble.

But that fear too would come to subside.

The last flash flood—a sudden Code Red a few weeks ago—arrived on a Tuesday and the sluices came down while Ivor was still at school. But during the one before that, back in late January, he was down by the Marsh when the sluices were closed. Then, as today, Jean was out looking for him around the Old City. She ended up walking along the top of the Walls, umbrella over her, studying the streets below to see sign of him in his red raincoat. As the rain grew heavier, it got harder to see. Her heart jumped when she thought she spotted him below, only to realise, a moment later, that what she had seen was only a post box, morphed and melted to her eyes by the thick rain.

Her phone buzzed and Jean struggled, with wet, nervous hands, to fish it out of her raincoat pocket before it rang out.

"He's with us up here," Angela O'Neill said on the other end of the line. The O'Neills were old neighbours of Jean's from her Irish Town days and well-loved by Ivor. The rain was hitting the umbrella hard and although Jean could hear Angela perfectly, she used the noise as a pretext to let the anxiety flow out of her.

"Sorry, Angela, you said he's safe and sound? He's fine? Is he fine?"

A positive response came across the line. Jean scraped her nail on the umbrella pole.

"Are you sure?"

The floodwaters had come in so fast that Ivor was cut off from his usual way home. He'd had to leave the Marsh in the opposite direction, by making his way up the hill towards Irish Town, across the way from the Old City.

Now, a dangerous channel of roaring water separated him from his mother. With all the sluice gates down and the Old City surrounded, Ivor would spend two days with the O'Neills before the currents weakened enough for the Flood Time Ferry Service to be started up.

During those two nights apart, Jean had visions of Ivor with his jar down by the Marsh, looking for fresh frogspawn. What was it in the search for spawn that had made him oblivious to the Code Orange, deaf to the sluice sirens coming from the Old City above?

In the darkness of her bedroom, with the faint sound of her other son, Joe's, video games coming through the wall, she imagined Ivor in his wellies and bright red raincoat, crouched over the fecund pools of the Marsh as the waters moved in silently around him.

In some visions, she trapped him with no way out, perched on a tuft of harder soil as the waters lapped ever closer, licking out at him as he trembled on his ledge—a newborn calf, alarmed yet ignorant of any response other than total submission to the great force of Nature bearing in around him.

Other scraps of visions lingered: Ivor knocked from his ledge and carried in the great currents of the flood. The futility of his efforts to tread water, the sound of his pathetic bleats, the certain death all made the brief images impossible—even for her—to sustain.

Last month, after three years spent in Year Seven, Ivor's form teacher told Jean that her son was now ready to make the move to secondary school. He would no longer be able to manage in mainstream education. In September, he'd be going to the Special School up on the Buncrana Road.

Jean could imagine a scared, forlorn Ivor standing in the yard on his first day in the new school, surrounded by other Special Kids—some in the same way as him but far worse; others epileptics, cerebral palsy kids, teenagers with Down's. The only remedy to the distress this image brought was to harbour irrational fantasies: that Ivor's growth would mysteriously halt, that he would stay in Year Seven for ever.

But already he stands high above his classmates, most of whom are a good three years his junior. The growth spurt came suddenly last year and brought with it the beginnings of a striking beauty in Ivor—a nuance of manhood that was the first manifestation Jean had seen of Ivor's father since he left a decade ago. This distinct beauty shot through to secret depths in her.

***

The bells of St. Augustine's ring out four times as Jean walks. Dusk won't be long. And then darkness.

Before the last peal fully dissipates, the Old City's Flood Sirens crank up into their slow wail. This particular tone signals that the sluice gates will come down in one hour. Jean swears under her breath. She's reached a part of the Wall beloved by Ivor, its tallest stretch in the whole city.

Last week he stood here, the unknowing subject of amorous glances from a group of teenage girls on a school trip to the Wall from St. Bridget's. Jean saw how his cool oblivion put sparkles in their eyes. His own eyes, though, remained in deep congress with a piece of moss growing on a snag some eight feet up the Wall.

Of late, this spot had become a site of pilgrimage for him, a place where he would study the Wall's many textures, running his hands along their regularity. Did that expanse of crisscrossed cement lines and recurring patterns of brick hold secret meanings for the palms of his hands? What were the Walls telling him?

Ivor's affinity with patterns and regularity had found a new expression in a deepening fascination with Nature and the processes of life that Nature lays bare. He'd pay special attention to how things intersected and cooperated in the natural world, how everything was ultimately interdependent. He could stand, enthralled, looking at the way a specific branch of a tree joined and fused with the trunk.

After the late-winter thaw, Ivor's Year Seven teacher took the class to the Marsh to study the "first signs of spring" in the water pools and on the earth tufts there. Ivor returned home in high excitement with a jam jar of frogspawn. He was so intrigued by it that he would sleep with the jar beside his bed and then, in the morning, he'd place it at his bedroom window so the spawn could catch as much light as possible while he was at school.

On getting home, he'd race directly to his room, drop his bag on his bed and go straight to the windowsill, hunkering down to gaze at the hundreds of little black eyes staring back at him from the spawn—all potentially on the brink of an as-yet-invisible metamorphosis.

When the black dots eventually did begin to lengthen, Ivor's joy, his unselfconscious whooping and jumping around his room, was so raw that it struck a fear in Jean. Soon, the black dots would stop elongating. No tadpoles would ever hatch. The spawn would die and turn rancid, she knew, and it would have to be disposed of.

***

They made a ceremony of it. They walked hand-in-hand up Society Street with the jar under Ivor's free arm. They turned silently onto Bishop Street Within, crossed the Diamond and stopped at the Wall at Shopquay Gate, the one that's permanently sealed up. They took the narrow stone stairs up onto the top of the Wall. Ivor peered over its edge down to the rapid waters of the Foyle sweeping along its outer side. He gasped weakly and jerked back with fright.

"Ah, son," said Jean. She pulled him close and took the jar from under his arm. She placed it on the Wall.

"Now," she nudged him. "Off with it."

Ivor unscrewed the jar lid. They said a quiet prayer together and then he poured the dead spawn into the raging waters below.

Later, with the jar washed and dried, Jean took Ivor, as promised, back to the Marsh to find more frogspawn so he could try, once again, to provide the love needed for those black dots on his windowsill to transform into the tadpoles and frogs that Nature had designed them to become.

At the Bishop's Gate exit, which leads to the Marsh, Ivor turned to Jean.

"Let me go on my own," he said. "I want to go on my own."

Leaning against the stone arch of the Gate, Jean watched as her son picked his way down the steep Bog Lane—jar under one arm, his glowing, energetic figure standing out against the muddy mid-March colours of the landscape beyond.

The Marsh had been made a Nature Preserve since the mass clearances of the '40s and '50s. As a girl, Jean used to play there in streets that no longer exist, used to attend birthday parties in back kitchens of houses long since razed. To the right of her field of vision, the Marsh gave way to the beginnings of the Bogside Channel, which wrapped out of view, around to the furious thrust of the Foyle on the other side of the Old City. Down under the Bogside Channel, somewhere, was her childhood home on Tyrconnel Street.

The Flood of '35 happened before Jean was even born but it had been a wake up call for all of Derry. Initially, a high watermark was set—a thick copper band, implanted into the slopes surrounding the city as a kind of monument. Sometimes, on summer evenings of her childhood, it used to catch rays from the setting sun and cast sharp glints of light down on Jean as she played in the streets of the Bogside. At the time, she'd fancy that the band of copper, throbbing as it was with fiery light, was a part of the hill's insides that had been exposed by some unexpected, violent gash and that those pulses of late-summer evening light were a private code of pain that the hill was communicating only to her. She was 11 when her family moved up to Irish Town, the new settlement up on the hill.

The demolition of the Bogside took years. During an initial period, when the area was cordoned off, it seemed like nothing was changing. The houses and streets stood just as they had been before, only now devoid of life. Former Bogsiders took to going to the Walls of the Old City for a view of their former homes, but this practice began to stop once the houses showed signs of dilapidation and decay. It came as a relief the day the demolition works finally made it to Tyrconnel Street. The seasonal floods had made the old houses sad and discoloured and, once they were razed, people could start the work of resurrecting them in their minds.

Then, one year, the seasonal floods never receded. The Bogside Channel was born.

In those early days—she was still living with her parents, before her marriage, before Joe, before Ivor—Jean would also go across to the Old City to gaze down at the Bogside Channel from the Walls. Back then, she could easily re-impose the old streets, specific houses, monuments and recollections onto the canvas of water below.

Now, when Jean looks down at the waters of the Channel, she struggles to see past the pleasure seekers and power walkers to discern the former Bogside topography beneath. All that come back easily are random, disconnected details: the garish yellow and orange wallpaper with the large, embossed flowers along the stairs; the missing key in the door of the bathroom; that one pane in the girls' bedroom window, broken by a rock and covered up with taut plastic. It all faded, so slowly that she barely noticed, like the sound of the voice of a deceased loved one: the fondness for them remains but the specifics of who they were—the timbre of their voice, their particular smell, their unique way of moving—fade into obscurity.

Ivor had reached the Marsh and was navigating his way through the waterlogged earth, jumping from one clump of hard earth to the next. Now he was hunkering down by a boggy pool, inspecting a part of it intently. He moved about on the spot a little bit before settling into an immobile, hunched-over posture.

Jean set out down the Bog Lane to get him. At one point on the descent, she stopped and looked beyond his still figure, up at the intersecting slopes around Derry. At certain spots, she could just about make out traces of the dirty track of the Copper Band, that once-gleaming high watermark of her childhood. It was the limit below which no house would ever be built in the future, city officials had said. Now it was barely visible, tarnished and muck-strewn after many floods, long forgotten and superseded by newer watermarks.

When she got close to Ivor, she could see his back shaking with giddiness.

"Son?"

"Mam." He turned to her, beaming. "They're alive! Look!"

She knelt beside him and looked into the pool. In it, among the clumps of spawn, were dozens of tadpoles darting about frenetically, some of them feeding on the unhatched spawn. In the jar of water sitting beside him on the pool's edge were a dozen tadpoles Ivor had scooped out.

The same routine of care developed as before. The jar of twelve tadpoles stayed by his bed at night. In the morning, he placed them by the window. After school, he rushed to the window to check on their progress.

There were signs of growth initially, but over the past three days a suspicion has come: that the growth is halting. Now, Jean can't shake the idea.

She's reached their home and opens the apartment door. No sign of Ivor.

"Ivor? Ivor, are you there?"

Silence. She waits.

She puts on the kettle. She looks for her phone. She puts away a plate that has been left out.

She hears the front door go. Runs to it.

"Ivor?"

It's Joe.

He starts talking about the café being shut early. The Code Orange. About getting paid for the full shift nonetheless. Jean's barely listening.

Poor Joe; it's not his fault. He has always known which one of them is her favourite... if disaster were to strike and she had to choose... before he was born, before he was conceived even, it was always Ivor.

Joe drones on as she walks into Ivor's room. On the window ledge, the jar. On the water's surface, twelve dead tadpoles.

***

Jean is panting by the time she reaches Bishop's Gate. The city workers are already making preparations for the lowering of the sluice. She walks out through the portal onto the top of the Bog Lane.

Down below is Ivor in his red raincoat, lying on the ground, his head bent down looking into a pool. Around him, the other pools of the marsh have grown from their usual sizes and are beginning to merge.

"Ivor," Jean calls out with blood in her voice. "Ivor."

Beyond his own rain-shattered reflection on the pool's surface swim baby frogs and some remaining tadpoles who have grown the beginnings of legs. They have already shed their blackness for a murky shade of green.

Ivor extends his fingers and touches the surface of the water. He pushes his open-spread hand down into the darkness of the pond and feels, with exhilaration, a current through his fingers. The currents have always been there. The coming flood has just pushed them to the point where he can feel them: a secret revealed. Born as they are of the scary, angry river, these currents are what bring life to the Marsh. They carry that pulse which ushers the spawn onto its awesome transformation. Everything is connected. Out here, there can be no fear. This is where love is.

Ivor is so close to the water's surface now that with a slight dip of his head, his face is submerged. Now, he can see the frogs and late-stage tadpoles in their own world, and beyond them, the further depths of the pool as it extends into darkness.

When Ivor's face pushes down into the water, Jean's back is turned. The last siren has started and she's looking at the Sluice Gate workers, wondering if she has enough time to run down the Bog Lane and get Ivor back up before the gates are fully shut.

In this moment of panicked calculation comes a familiar anxiety. It reminds her of Ivor's birth, fourteen years ago. The labour was long and ended in an emergency caesarean. High on oxygen, under strong local anaesthetic and curtained off from what the doctors were doing, Jean felt—at the moment of incision—a sudden release of pressure in her abdomen, a deluge out of her.

Turning away from the Sluice Gate workers, Jean makes to run down the Bog Lane but stops when she sees that Ivor has ducked his head into the water.

Down below, he can feel frogs' feet brush his cheeks and

tadpoles swim in and through his hair. He could be swimming with them, she thinks. Discovering that silent world with his frogs. She sees him move gracefully with them through the weeds and silt, moving deeper and deeper until they reach a place he only knows intuitively, through her. 34 Tyrconnel Street. He swims through the front door and past the garish orange and yellow wallpaper on the stairs. He stops for a moment and takes one of the large, embossed, yellow flowers out from the wallpaper, continuing to float on up the stairs, past the key-less bathroom door and into Jean's bedroom where she is sitting on her bed, weeping. The wardrobes are empty. A suitcase lies next to her feet. Ivor sits beside her, wipes the tears from her cheeks and hands her the flower. Taking her hand, he swims up off the bed, leading her to the small window frame covered in plastic. Together they peel it off and, as it bobs and pirouettes to the floor, the boy and girl swim out through the window and far away.

The last wail of the siren dies out. Jean is running down the Bog Lane when Ivor's head crashes back up from the water. He gasps for air and turns, looking up at her. His face is fresh, flushed from the cold. His cheeks shimmer from the water flowing down over them.

They hold their positions, looking at each other. The old love seeps back in, found again. With it, a new estrangement begins to assert its force.

Research for this story and an initial draft of the text were undertaken in the context of a workshop called "Ecotopian Derry-Londonderry," run by Queen's University Belfast in Derry city in August 2018.

Anne McCrea

bog people

Sunday   I walk the bogs of Donegal
think of the bog people   their last
meal
undigested millet husks and blackberries

one with hair gel to make him seem
taller
the Tollund man eulogised by Heaney
bog cotton   sphagnum moss

the ground gives under your boots
out here anything could happen
a blow to the head   a slip over a cliff

we make our way round the peninsula
and once in a while meet   a farmer
living on the edge

Seth Crook

Daily Swim

A precise *A* to *B*.
  From your clothes dump
back to your clothes dump.

Turning at a moored boat,
  a pink or yellow buoy,
a nearby kelp-bearded island.

Walking out of the water
  always feels like a mini-triumph.
A garland of sea lace.

If you take some sand away,
  toed inside your socks,
you can stand on the beach all day.

Mark Baker

Sunny Spell

What of lace-flowers, dusk's pinks
and mosses emerald furs for a taste of wild honey?
Let fuchsia be scarlet,
the souls of children first come as bees.
Think it not overmuch, she said
lost behind closed eyes
while lupines stretched like for like
as bodies and dreams of the poppy's blush
and she was within the plants
where I'd walked fearing cancer, apocalypse.
What if I entered the strangeness of another's story
pulsing to the laughter of time and learnt
I wasn't who I thought I was,
my cheeks brushed with those dusts' soft splendours,
with permission to be beautiful in lavender and rosemary,
my nose a celebrant of air?
Too drowsy and drugged and dim
I am of pollens,
gifted with fuzz and blur
in the warmth of the hug that has split the seed-caps,
rim, cup and skin
turning into the throats of birds:
welcomes, warnings
then sudden gone-to-ground quietness
my surrender too
when at last,
it's rain.

Marc Swan

Wild About Wampum

Marcia walks us through history in four thousand pieces.
We are ensnared by the verbal web
of this strong-willed woman—
small-boned, muscular, face and arms
covered in fine white dust,
gray-blonde hair pulled back,

green painted toenails poking out of sandals.
She walks with us down a narrow hallway.
Perched on a stool in the corner beneath
a filtration system
inside a glass-walled room, a Mi'kmaq woman
sits, dremel in hand guiding

a thin drill bit through
a thick white shell lowered
into a tray of water.
Her respirator hums. Marcia stands
by our side describing equipment,
process, stockpile of various sized quahogs.

She explains,
she's not native, but loves the possibilities
of wampum.
We ask questions, nod and smile.
A crow flutters from a window perch

to the couch, to the counter.
He was injured a month ago,
has since settled
into this new home. He spends his days
looking at other birds out the window,

hiding earrings left on tables.
In the gallery Marcia
presents her creations:
some exotic, some mundane,
and seems pleased to have an audience.
At one point, she drops

the right shoulder of her tee, displays
a purple and white
bigger-than-life quahog
tattoo. She tells us
she dreams in purple and white.
She plans to have her ashes

scattered in a quahog bed. Her only fear
is a tomahawk war—
First Nation neighbors who hold her in mixed regard
breaking down the door.

Paul Lewis

Salthill Littoral

Chief Types of Clouds, from high to low:

cirrostratus: uniform milky layer of high sheet cloud, sun shines through with a distinctive halo; almost certain bad weather.

cirrocumulus: formed of ice crystals, lines of small globular masses with rippled appearance, with blue sky between (mackerel sky); approaching bad weather.

cirrus: delicate, fibrous, wispy, consisting of tiny ice particles; often indicates bad weather. If drawn out in "mare's tail" it indicates strong winds in the upper atmosphere.

cumulonimbus: develops in a great vertical height, upper part anvil-like, thundercloud; torrential rain or hail, black from below, from the side a great silvery mass.

altostratus: greyish, uniform sheet, sun is seen as through ground glass; approaching rain.

altocumulus: fleecy, cellular cloud, separated by blue sky; fair weather.

nimbostratus: low dark cloud; continuous rain.

cumulus: cloud which grows vertically from a flat base into large rounded summits.

stratocumulus: uniform, heavy cloud; often covers the sky for long dreary periods in winter.

stratus: heavy, grey, uniform, low-lying sheet of cloud; often very persistent and sometimes giving continuous drizzling rain.

Sundry Key Notes and Terms:

knotted wrack: brown seaweed, amongst various wracks (bladder, channelled); found at about half-tide.

neap tide: reduced tide when gravitational attraction of the sun and moon are in opposition to each other.

spring tide: one of the tides of greatest range; occurs when the moon, sun and earth, in conjunction or opposition, are in the same straight line; happens twice a month, after full and new moons.

littoral: of, on, near the shore, esp. land lying between high and low tide.

synygy: the conjunction or opposition when the sun, moon and earth are in the same line.

apogee: the point in the orbit of the moon when it is at its furthest distance from the earth.

nimbus: cloud from which rain falls.

pluvial: of rain; rainy.

nebula: a cloud of interstellar matter.

star: globe of incandescent gas, very remote.

celestial: of the sky

Note also: The Seven Seas, The Four Winds, The Sands of Time and The Lonesome Moon.

...and alas;
The tide went out
                                        The clouds moved in
                                        The rain came down
                                        The clouds moved around
                                        The sun went down
                                        The tide came in
The sky cleared up
                                        The moon came out
                                        The stars came out
                                        The wind picked up
                                        The tide went out
The sun came up
The wind died down

                                        The wracks waft
                                        The ocean swells
                                        The sands shift

And life
continues
dwindling on
the tilting Earth

Michael Phoenix

The Dogs

Paul and I grew up being driven through town with my Da at our red van's wheel. The dogs grew up on the seat behind us, the male Paul's and the girl, mine.

Ma left when I was eight and Paul a few years older. It was early summer. She took a room in a shared house just onto the hill west of town. After she went she called us, and after a moment, after I answered, she asked me for Paul. I'm not sure of everything that she told him, but about the house she left to I am, for Paul, he shouted it out.

An old pair lit the place up for her. They rubbed their freckled sleeves together at morning and sneezed chalkish the afternoon and at evening told stories about when they were kids and they rowed through grass fields and when they were wild-haired, stoic, pebble-footed adventurers and middle-aged, waterproof alder trees and how they sung without loving and danced and danced in the cave of love.

Not long after the call Paul started to struggle to sleep, and when he couldn't sleep he would often talk about Ma. It might have only been the way that memories are voiced, translated piece-by-piece into the palate of the person whose spirit fills them up, but those nights gripped me. I remember one thing he said most clearly, because as he began to say it the frame in the window at the bottom of our shared room, and the dirt that covered the window until the rain came and changed the town, was cutting a blood moon into tiny star-like pieces that fell through the glass and mixed amongst his words, turning them into unreal things that I know never meant what they should have to me. She walked with her head swaying, he said. Her eyes were too stone-like and mad for all the looking about that she wanted to do. It was that kind of looking that let her see the dog. It was wandering out on the back hill of town—and I was there with her then—we found him. And when we did she threw her hands out to him like she could have held off the future if she'd wanted to. That saved him. It's her dog really, more than mine.

I didn't join in when he talked about her like that. I listened but I grew without her, and now when I think of her I only really think of Paul's stories. There's just one true image I have. She sits in the front room, on the arm of one of my Da's wicker chairs, and looks down at Paul's dog on the rug in the middle of the floor, and where my dog is I don't know. Then she lifts her eyes and drifts them to Paul. He sits against the pale wall opposite reading a book she bought of animal stories bound in a dark red cover. I can't be sure if it's a true memory. I don't know if I only look in on it or if I am somewhere in the picture. I might be Paul and Ma and the dog and the book and the stories in it, but I was never a part of any of the things that existed between them.

My Da and I walked to the lake evenings that summer. We went one day with willow branches bundled cross us. We paused at one moment to balance them, and I asked him why Ma had left. The question had always been missing a piece and even then I'm not sure it was full. It had taken me a long time to form it and it took my Da a long time to answer. It wasn't until a few days later that he finally did. We were passing through the town square, semi-circling around the grey stock-dove fountain when he tried to explain what it means to linger.

My Da was a good man. He had bark hands and soily eyes and I thought that if I asked him to he would put nails through them for me. Now and then, even after Ma left, he would laugh from amongst the softest of openings. The leaves of his laughter would push out of him and wing through the windows of our house and over the cuts of our hard dirt path and move off down the road and out into the rest of the world. Paul might have talked about Ma at night, but I dreamt of my Da. Sometimes I saw him walk past me, off into a distance out away from town, and a long time would go by, years or decades or centuries of dream. I would panic and become breathless, then wake up burnt out, like an animal lost in the night.

When our neighbour came to tell us the police had arrested Paul, my Da made his body very still. He asked the man what it was to do with, and when he heard it was about Ma he thanked the neighbour for coming and then stood holding onto the frame of the front door with one hand, thinking, I thought, of what might have been happening to both of them then. And in the space opened by that moment in which he didn't think of me, something strong, something opaque, came and started to gather.

Da closed the front door, then left the hall. He disappeared into the small room under the trap to the attic, and I wanted to move too but couldn't. I stayed where I was, at the limit between our home and the hall. Something measured down the length of my bones. When he reappeared he had his red rain jacket on. He told me he was going to get Paul and that I should stay home, and although I could move once he had spoken, I didn't know how to shake off whatever it was I had seen and felt. I wanted to go with him. I wanted to search for Ma and Paul. But in an instant, my Da had gone.

At some point that night the dogs appeared. At first it seemed there was only Paul's, but slowly he separated, splitting into two, and my dog was there alongside. I watched them from a huddle up on the wicker chair, and for a moment only saw the fine spaces between the edges of their hair and the soot collecting in the fireplace behind them. Then I realised that one of them had been crying. I couldn't be sure which one it was, and I don't know why, but I didn't want to stand from the chair and move closer to find out. Finally, the girl uncurled herself and I saw that the cry had been hers. She began to whimper until her aches pyramided into a high-pitched noise that was not a cry anymore but the sound of her digging into herself, and I ran at the other dog, lashing out with my limbs and teeth.

Three hours later Da came back. Paul was a step behind him. Both of them were soaking wet. The whites of their eyes were dirty. I stood in front of the hall and stared at them till the dog rushed past me and threw himself onto the floor before Paul, staining the hall-stones with blood that drifted out amongst the wet dirt breaking from their shoes as they entered.

Paul stared at me then. He stared till he saw through me. That's how the rain began.

The town was a patchwork of cobble, shop and animal noise and the rain turned it to mud. On days when the sun fought through the clouds we could see the roots of our houses breaking up between the street-stones and gasping for air between the bursts of rain. Maybe it fell for six months or a year before we began to pull wet saws through the wet orange light of the street lamps, cutting damp branches from willow trees into human forms, and in the mornings put on rain boots and hoods to carry them through the gate of the yard in the ash tree end of town. Paul had been gone all the first morning that Da was called to help. Da had stood in the doorway looking out for him for a long while before he made to leave. As he stood there I got up from the wicker chair in the front room and moved to hand him his red rain jacket. He didn't turn when I spoke to him or when I held the jacket out, but only stepped away from the house and looked up then down the road to town, stretched his arm back and lifted the jacket over his neck and shoulders, colouring the rainfall red and sending it sliding cold and heavy into my eyes so that for a long time thereafter, until I left the town too, at times I felt as though that coloured rain were running through me in the places where my blood should have been and I were rusting for it finitely, like a doomed clock motor.

We waxed cross the holes in our wooden doors, thickened our windows with poster paper, and covered our floors in rugs Da wove from hair Paul's dog shed. The orders for his woven chairs and his woven baskets stopped, so he made more rugs for our neighbours. They would come to the front door to collect them and talk or gossip until their running out of words hit against the walls inside our house like wet matches striking the sides of their boxes and Da sat still. Sometimes stray cars would tear down the road to town like thunder bolts through the quietude. And the days when we would ride around in the red van echoed after them. Paul went out walking with his dog for hours on end. He never asked me to join him. He never even let us know where he would go. It was like neither the rain nor we existed.

After he was taken to the barracks, Paul stopped talking about Ma. Soon after he began to leave our room in the night, walking in his sleep. He would explore the house when he did, going right up into the corners in short child-like steps, and write notes wherever he found scraps of paper, on newspapers or envelopes or posters or parts of the wallpaper scratched down by his dog. Sometimes it would only be a line of something he was dreaming or something with no sense in it at all, but now and then he would rain out stories, scrawled but fierce and legible.

I went back not long ago and the house is still there. It was odd, and I don't really understand it for there's only one person it could have been, but each one of those notes of Paul's was collected, and they were stained and creased from folding and unfolding and reading and rereading. I took them up when I found them. They still belong to that opaque place for things that I've never truly been part of.

One day, he wrote, the rain was displaced by sleet and hail, and overnight a freeze on the lake began. Over a week its colour transformed as the layer of ice on its surface sank and expanded and darkened. And it was solid for a month before it began to change again. Then, the hail rewound into sleet and the sleet melted back to rain and a bright day came, then a bright morning. A warm wind carried a crack splintering towards town, sounding twists on the muddy paths that lead in from the lake and crying out like a chain of crashing cars when it met the hard dirt and stone streets of town, and reached the door of a house where a woman lived and stopped in its wood like a dead arrow.

I don't know where that story came from, or whether it was a story at all. It wasn't something I had heard before. The lake froze once or twice, maybe, and melted back later, but maybe it was only a dream, something unique to him. About the woman, I don't know.

One morning Da said there was a place he had to go and asked if I might go with him.

We drove cross town to a shop that had sent post and sold useful and unuseful things right through to the middle of the rain. As we drew up the shop seemed to be closed, but Da pulled up the zipper on his red rain jacket and left the van all the same. He pushed through the shop's front door with the flat of his hand and disappeared a dream-like while. I sat in the van, leaning towards the windscreen, and although I shouldn't have been able to, to begin with I could listen after him in spite of the rain. Da's voice, mixed in with others, came from the front of the shop, and I could see movement through gaps in the curtains cross its windows. But then the movements fell away and the voices went with them, and the rain began to fall more thickly until it piled up over the van's windows and filled me with a nervous fear and I could see nothing but it; I was in it and it was a nightmare. Ma had become Paul and he had become Da and they had walked away from me. Then the dog cried. I sat up on my knees and turned to look at her. She made that noise again as if she were digging into herself and no one seemed to hear her for no one came to help us. I felt that fear in the rain around me turning into something else, turning into sleet and turning into hail, and I struck out at her, bruising the backseat, until she became silent and still but for her belly rising and falling like water moving into sand, and her breath graced cross my hands like the physical thing it stemmed from was about to expire

and for a second I could not see the dog at all
and the rain hailed against me
cutting me red,

until I heard a swing, the shop door opening,
and she was gone.

Toby Buckley

Inver

In the bay there were five or six
great dark floating monsters—
fish farms tended by men in RIBs
who threw down illegal lobster pots
and slung us Tesco bags of crab claws
not to tout. Our teas-with-powdered-milk
and cuppa soup cup dinners
all tasted like boat, like purple
methylated spirits too pretty
to drink, and the dolphins all had gaps
and chunks missing and looked wrong and wild
and not like the real dolphins I saw
on TV. And their wet backs brushed
slimey against our feet and in school
I lied and made them magic,
kept the truth in the boot with the lifejackets.

Aoife Riach

Priorities

When the tides come pounding
on the glassfront office block,
overwatering the potted plant till its leaves
blister and burst and mouldering
the freshly vacuumed carpet,
who will we scold for opening the window?

Wading through sea-swaddled stationery
bobbing past the laminator, and swamped boxes
of headed paper, in pours our inexorable end.

Refusing to grasp the gravity of the gravity
that floats filing cabinets along the ocean floor
of polystyrene cups and post-its,
still my head snaps up.

Strung to the scald of flesh between your jumper
and jeans as you reach and carve the waterline,
your shoulder thrust to glass, forcing it
shut, stemming the flow, granting us a sodden,
surplus minute.

Celia Claase

Cylinder Creature

Here I am,
in the time of strange
little creatures.

A fast moving one,
thick as my arm, grown out of a
spiralled spine, slides across flat surfaces
and bends sharply around corners.

It stretches far and shrinks small.

Babies burst from its
hunched backbone.

Pete Mullineaux

Boarders

A scuffling in the bushes. I soften my breathing and wait...
until a perfect Brock face emerges from the dark—and
then another rough shape reverses out of the compost
heap, looking like a tangled up hairbrush. After a few
moments of nosing they both melt back into the shadows.

I feel privileged. Does this mean they'll be staying?
Cousins to otter, mink, pine martin, wolverine!
I've heard how they trample down flowers, will make
a golf course of the lawn rooting for grubs. Perhaps if
I learn some of their language we can set up a dialogue,
come to a reasonable compromise over rights of way and

borders; find some natural accommodation. Who knows,
with all that digging, those squat snouts may even unearth
a poem or two.

Lisa Reily

in a bath with Bruce Dawe

you and I
in a bath and in love,
only months after we met;
moved in together too soon,
they said,
in front and behind our backs.
we did it anyway.
warm water around us, bubbles long faded
we lean into Sunday,
rest in each other's space,
read poetry together:
Bruce Dawe;
our little dog Henry on the bathmat
loyally waits.
we splash him for fun and he bites at the water,
the tiles growing slippery as he runs
back-and-forth
back-and-forth
skips, barks, spins, skids
until he falls
a fall
that took a part of me,
forever.
his little legs splayed, he stops,
unable to move.
for days after, you carried him
up and down our stairs,

held him gently on your lap;
each day you sat, still and silent,
so he slept
unaffected by your movements;
watching you,
I knew you were the one.

Cliona O'Connell

Tornado

Sultry all day, the crowds have retired to their snoring
or to tearing one another asunder.
From the whitewashed bar, the last along the coast road,
the twister looks benign,
painted even, tidy brush strokes
in textured creams and accents:
if it moves it does so slyly. Not a breath
of wind in it today
you might conjure the dead to say;
now don't breathe a word of it.
As a man pours a drink into silence
a gecko lightens itself along a wall,
a word like a charge
roars itself across the sea;
no one can hear it yet,
not the barman,
not the gecko,
not me.

Cliona O'Connell

Whites and Shadows

"ar scáth a chéile a mhairimíd."

A larger than life
silhouette on the bank

has Balsam leaves
in its head

The torso is semi see-through
made of soft troughs

of malleable, mucky earth
and a skim of water

reflects light stories
of the leaves on the trees overhead

White butterflies gather
and scatter on it

settle and flicker
in a skittish, girlish flutter

This shadow is old
but I am younger

I am filled with a talent
for laughter

as we live in the shelter
of each other

Notes on Contributors

Mark Baker is a Dublin-based poet. In 2009 he was selected for Poetry Ireland's Introduction Series. In 2015 he won the Listowel Writer's Week Poetry Collection competition. He has been published in *The Stinging Fly*, *The Shop*, *West 47* and *The Poetry Ireland Review*.

Amanda Bell's publications include *the loneliness of the sasquatch* (Alba Publishing, 2018), *First the Feathers* (Doire Press, 2017), *The Lost Library Book* (The Onslaught Press, 2017), and *Undercurrents* (Alba Publishing, 2016). She is assistant editor of *The Haibun Journal*. www.clearasabellwritingservices.ie @gagebybell

David Butler's second poetry collection, *All the Barbaric Glass*, was published in 2017 by Doire Press. His poem-cycle 'Blackrock Sequence', a Literary Arts Commission illustrated by his brother Jim, won the World Illustrators Award 2018. Poetry prizes include the Féile Filíochta, Ted McNulty, Brendan Kennelly, Poetry Ireland / Trocaire and Baileborough awards.

Toby Buckley is a trans writer from Donegal, currently based in Glasgow. He completed his MA in poetry at Queen's University Belfast, and has been published in *The Tangerine*, *Poetry Ireland Review* and *The Stinging Fly*, as well as a number of different independent zines.

Jan Carson is a writer and community arts facilitator based in East Belfast. She has a novel, *Malcolm Orange Disappears*, and short story collection, *Children's Children*, (Liberties Press), a micro-fiction collection, *Postcard Stories* (Emma Press). Her novel *The Fire Starters* was published by Doubleday in 2019. It won the EU Prize for Literature for Ireland 2019.

Celia Claase is a South African-born writer and co-founder of Blank Page Writers' Forum Hong Kong. Her first full length collection of poems, *The Layers Between*, received the 2014 International Proverse Prize. Her poems have since appeared in several print and online publications, including *New Coin*, *Scrutiny2*, *LitNet*, *Sarie Magazine* and *Imprint*.

John Creevy grew up in Mayo. He has a Masters in Creative Writing from Trinity College. In 2018 he was a young writer delegate for the Dublin Book Festival. He is currently teaching in Dublin while writing short stories in his spare time. He is also involved with Fighting Words Ireland.

Lucy Crispin's work has appeared in *Envoi*, *Eildon Tree*, *Allegro*, *The Quiet Feather, The Selkie*, *Iceberg Tales* and other magazines as well as in various anthologies. She works freelance for the Wordsworth Trust and as a person-centred counsellor. Her micro-pamphlet, *wish you were here*, is forthcoming from Hedgehog Press.

Seth Crook can see Ireland from the hill beside his house, has taught philosophy at various universities, lives in the Hebrides and is transitioning into a seal. His poems have most recently appeared in such places as *The Rialto*, *Southlight*, *Causeway*, *Magma*, *Envoi*, *Northwords Now*, *Antiphon*, *Stravaig*.

Martina Dalton lives in Tramore, County Waterford. Her

background is in visual art. She studied fine art at Waterford Institute of Technology, specialising in painting. Her poems have been published in *Poetry Ireland Review, The Stony Thursday Book*, *Crannóg*, and *Skylight 47*.

Born in Birkenhead, UK, **John Paul Davies** was second in the 2017 Waterford Poetry Prize, and third in the 2018 IT Tallaght Story Prize. His poems feature in *Southword*, *The Pedestal*, *Maine Review*, *Crannóg*, *Manchester Review* and *Abridged*. He's a member of The Bull's Arse Writers in Navan, Co. Meath (Twitter: @Bulls_Arse).

Patrick Deeley is from Loughrea, County Galway. His seventh collection of poems with Dedalus Press, *The End of the World*, has just been published. He is the recipient of the American-based Lawrence O'Shaughnessy Award for 2019.

When he isn't writing, or experimenting with film, **Colin Hopkirk** can either be found at the music charity where he works, or somewhere outside, with or without family, in nature. He used to sing in a DIY punk band that wasn't very good, but got away with it through sheer enthusiasm.

Joey Lew holds an MFA from UNC-Greensboro and is currently a medical student at UCSF. Her interviews and reviews have been published in *Diode*, *Michigan Quarterly Review Online*, and *Tupelo Quarterly*. Her poetry can be seen in *Gravel* and *Black Bough Poetry* and is forthcoming in *One*.

Paul Lewis comes from Cork City. He now lives in Galway, working as a chef, studying and writing some essays, poetry and short fiction.

D.S. Maolalai has been nominated for Best of the Web and twice for the Pushcart Prize. His poetry has been released in two collections, *Love is Breaking Plates in the Garden* (Encircle Press, 2016) and *Sad Havoc Among the Birds* (Turas Press, 2019).

Suzzanna Matthews recently completed a postgraduate degree in Creative Writing. While she considers California home, she spent a better part of her childhood in New England. She's lived and studied abroad in Latin America, Europe and Asia. She lives in Dublin, where she is working on a collection of short stories.

Anne McCrea lives in the North West Ireland. She has a degree in French from QUB and a Master's Degree in French Studies from the University of Ulster. She has had poems published by *North West Words*, *Nine Muses Poetry* and work included in community led arts initiatives in Strabane.

Pete Mullineaux lives in Galway. He's published four poetry collections, most recently *How to Bake a Planet* (Salmon 2016). His work has been published internationally in a number of eco-journals. He's also had several plays produced for radio. Pete teaches awareness of global issues in schools, using poetry and drama.

Cliona O'Connell's debut collection of poetry, *White Space*, was published in 2012. She has been runner-up in the Patrick Kavanagh Award, selected for Poetry Ireland Introductions and shortlisted for the Hennessey Literary Awards. Cliona has a Masters in Poetry Studies from Dublin City University and a Masters in Creative Writing from Trinity College Dublin.

Karen O'Connor is winner of the Listowel Writers' Week Single Poem Prize, the Allingham Poetry Award, the Jonathan Swift Creative Writing Award for Poetry and the Nora Fahy Literary Award for Short Story. Karen's second poetry collection, *Between The Lines*, was featured on RTE Radio 1 Arts Programme, Arena.

Don Ó Donnacháin is a native of Ballymahon, Co. Longford and currently lives in Belfast where he teaches journalism and broadcast storytelling at Queen's University. He has an interest in languages, folklore and mythology. He has made audio documentaries, sound art performances and short films. He is currently working on a sequence of short stories and a novel. www.donduncan.net

Michael Phoenix is a writer from Belfast. He has previously published short stories in *The Dublin Review* and *The Bohemyth*.

Lisa Reily is a former literacy consultant, dance director and teacher from Australia. Her poetry has been published in several journals, such as *Amaryllis*, *London Grip*, *Panoplyzine*, *Magma Poetry* and *Sentinel Literary Quarterly* magazine. You can find out more about Lisa at lisareily.wordpress.com

Aoife Riach is a queer feminist witch with an MPhil in Gender & Women's Studies. Her poetry has been published by *College Green Journal*, *Impossible Archetype* and other magazines. She was a 2019 Irish Writers Centre Young Writer Delegate and her poem 'Vancouver' was selected for the Hungering curation of the Poetry Jukebox.

Lola Scollard is a member of the Seanchai Writers Group in Listowel. Her poetry has appeared in *Still in the Dreaming* 2018 and *Seashores Haiku Journal*. She was an award winner at the Poetry Competition in Ballydonghue 2019. Originally from West Clare, she now lives in Kerry.

Lisa Stice is a poet/mother/military spouse. She is the author of two full-length collections, *Permanent Change of Station* (Middle West Press, 2018) and *Uniform* (Aldrich Press, 2016), and a chapbook, *Desert* (Prolific Press). She currently lives in North Carolina with her husband, daughter and dog. lisastice.wordpress.com / twitter: @LisaSticePoet / facebook.com/LisaSticePoet

Marc Swan is a retired vocational rehabilitation counselor. His poems have recently been published in *Ropes*, *Crannóg*, *Gargoyle*, *The Broadkill Review*, among others. *today can take your breath away*, his fourth collection, was published in 2018 by Sheila-na-gig Editions. He lives with his wife Dd in coastal Maine.

Ojo Taiye is a young Nigerian who uses poetry as a handy tool to hide his frustration with the society. His poem 'Elegiac' is the winner of the 2019 Hart Crane Poetry Prize. His writing has appeared in or is forthcoming from *Grist Journal*, *Fiddlehead*, *The Well Review*, *Lambda Literary*, *Glintmoon*, *Banshee*, *Ruminate*, *Savant-Garde Journal*, *Strange Horizon*, and elsewhere. You can find him on twitter @ojo_poems.

Rosamund Taylor won the Mairtín Crawford Award for poetry at the Belfast Book Festival in 2017, and has been nominated for a Forward Prize for best single poem. Her work has recently appeared in *Agenda*, *Banshee*, *Magma*, *Poetry Ireland Review* and on *LambdaLiterary.Org*.

Iain Twiddy studied literature at university and lived for several years in northern Japan. He has poems published or forthcoming in *The Poetry Review*, *Stand*, *Poetry Ireland Review*, *The Stinging Fly* and elsewhere.

Lydia Unsworth is the author of two collections of poetry: *Certain Manoeuvres* (Knives Forks & Spoons, 2018) and *Nostalgia for Bodies* (Winner, 2018 Erbacce Poetry Prize). Her latest pamphlet *My Body in a Country* is available to download from Ghost City Press. Recent work can be found in *Ambit*, *Litro*, *para.text*, *Tears in the Fence*, *Banshee*, *Riggwelter*, and others. Manchester / Amsterdam. Twitter@lydiowanie

Polly Waterfield has been the child of a diplomatic family, a professional violinist, a member of the Findhorn community, a Suzuki violin teacher, a printmaker, and an Alexander Technique teacher. In her 60s she has surprised herself by becoming involved with Extinction Rebellion.

Grace Wilentz's poetry has appeared in Irish, British and American journals including *Poetry Ireland Review*, *Cyphers*, *The Seneca Review*, *The American Poetry Journal*, *Magma*, *The Harvard Advocate*, and *The Irish Times*. Her debut pamphlet, *Holding Distance*, will be launched by the Green Bottle Press in October 2019.

Elspeth Wilson has an MPhil in Gender Studies and a particular interest in nature writing. She has recently started writing poetry; in 2019 her poems were shortlisted for the Streetcake Experimental Writing prize and nominated for Best of the Net. Her works-in-progress include a novel and her first poetry collection.